MW00911238

ANDREW DONKIN

The Bugman

Illustrated by Doffy Weir

MACDONALD YOUNG BOOKS

For Graham Brand

The Project

This was the thing he liked best. Making the decision. Deciding who he wanted to pick.

School was over for the day and as the other pupils came out, Justin was getting ready to spring his ambush. Justin was the tallest and biggest in his year and everyone was scared of him.

Justin watched from his hiding place as the smaller school kids streamed past him like ants.

Sometimes Justin stopped people for dinner money or sweets but today he had something quite special in mind. He needed to find somebody from this morning's Science class.

Finally, just as the last few pupils were drifting out of the school gates, he saw

Carl. Carl from the Science class. Carl in his bright new blazer. Carl.

6

As Carl walked past, Justin grabbed him.

"Get off," said Carl weakly as he saw who it was. Carl was used to this routine. Thinking quickly, he started to turn out his pockets to show that they were empty.

"That's not what I want," said Justin, lifting Carl up so that only his toes touched the pavement. "I want to swap Science projects," he explained.

"I've got a horrible one, insects. You know how many of those there are. You've got trees. How hard can that be? So we're swapping. Right? I'll do trees. You do insects."

"But what if I get in trouble for swapping?" pleaded Carl.

"You'll be in more trouble if you don't," said Justin, smiling as he pushed Carl through the hedge behind them.

The Nest

Justin sat in the local park. He was
munching on sweets he'd taken from the
other pupils. Justin was copying the names
of trees out of a text book, claiming to have
seen them all himself.

Justin looked around him. It was getting
dark. In the distance, a Park Keeper was
blowing his whistle, signalling for everyone
to leave.

Justin stood up and unwrapped another sweet. He carelessly let the sweet paper fall to the ground. As he did, he noticed a trail of bugs leading away from the other wrappers he had dropped.

The bugs were ugly but Justin was fascinated by them. He slowly followed the line of scurrying black beetles until he found their nest.

The large mound of sculptured earth looked strange and sinister under the final rays of the setting sun.

Justin felt his skin crawl as he watched dozens of shiny bugs running in and out of the nest. This was just the kind of thing Carl would need for his insect project. Justin checked around him.

A Park Keeper rode by on his bike. He
blew his whistle again. As soon as he was
out of sight, Justin raised his foot and
brought it down with a great thud onto the
side of the nest. The whole mound vibrated
but it did not break or even crack. Justin
kicked again …
and again.

By the time he had finished, his training
shoes were black. He had kicked the nest
into oblivion.

That night, Justin sank down into his soft
bed. It had been a good day.

Justin reached
across to turn off
his bedside lamp.
As his hand felt
for the switch, a
small black shape
scuttled away into
the shadows.
Justin did not see
it though. He was
soon asleep.

One Million Eggs

Next morning, Justin got ready for school.
He had stayed in bed too long and had to
rush to make up for lost time.

Justin got half his arm in his blazer and
was wiggling his foot into his trainer. He
had just pulled on his blazer properly when
– UGH! – he suddenly felt something in
his shoe.

14

Justin's heart jumped.
It must be a bug from
yesterday! He ripped his
shoe off, then picked up
a large book. Justin
slowly tipped up the offending shoe. He
held the book, ready to whack whatever
emerged. He tipped it further ... and
further. Suddenly it fell out. Justin watched
it hit the carpet. It was only a small stone.

At school, the first lesson after registration was Science. Mrs Dean went around the class asking how everyone's projects were coming along.

Justin surprised her by saying that his was nearly finished. Carl seemed much less happy when Mrs Dean asked him about his project.

At lunch-time, Justin headed out to the school playing field. A football game was in progress and there was a pile of school bags nearby.

Justin was hungry and someone was about to give him a free lunch. He spotted Carl's bag and opened it, taking out Carl's packed lunch.

Carl ran over to protest but it was too late. Justin had opened the sandwiches and had taken a deliberately big mouthful. Justin smiled at Carl as he enjoyed the lunch he had stolen.

Justin was chewing away when he suddenly froze. A bug's head had popped out of the uneaten half of the sandwich! Then the whole bug wiggled free!

Another bug appeared. Then another!
Justin's eyes stared in disgust!

"Yuuch!" he shrieked as he dropped the
sandwich in horror.

Everyone around
moved closer to see what was
happening. They saw the bugs crawl out of
the abandoned sandwich and started to
laugh at Justin.

First it was just a few
of them but then the
laughter seemed to
spread through the crowd like a wave.

"If you've swallowed one," said a voice
from the back, "it might lay a million eggs
inside your tummy and they'll all hatch and
crawl out!"

Everyone laughed. Everyone except
Justin. He rushed off to find a water
fountain.

20

That afternoon, Justin tried to pay
attention in class but it was very difficult.
All the time, he thought he could feel
something moving around in his stomach.
Something creepy. Something crawly. The
more he tried not to think
about it, the more
difficult it
got.

Justin had ended up not having any
lunch, so it was not very long before his
stomach started making strange noises
anyway.

What happened next was even worse.
The teacher pulled down the next section of
the revolving blackboard to find a clean
area.

On the board was a
chalk drawing of Justin
with bugs swarming
out of his mouth.

Someone had drawn it knowing that the teacher would pull it into sight sooner or later. When they caught sight of it, the whole class started laughing. Even the ones who had not been there at lunch-time.

Justin went red and ran for the door. No one had ever seen him move so fast.

The Creeping Fear

After school, as they headed home,
everybody caught up with the latest news
on Justin. They talked and joked about
what had happened.

From his hiding place, Justin watched the
smiling faces go past. His back had been
itching all afternoon. He scratched it again.
Where was Carl? This was all his fault.

Then Justin spotted Carl walking along
with the others. He was laughing as well.
Justin moved in quickly and grabbed hold
of him. He swung Carl round and pushed
him into a bush.
Carl fell to the
ground.

Now for revenge. Justin clenched his fists
and stepped forward. Suddenly he stopped
dead. His eyes bulged. He looked horrified,
then afraid.

Justin could go no closer to Carl. On the leaves of the bush above Carl's head were caterpillars. Lots of large, ugly caterpillars.

The insects were everywhere. One raised the front of its hairy segmented body and seemed to stare up at Justin.

Justin could not bring himself to go anywhere near the repulsive creatures and backed away. He left without saying a word and went home.

Justin had a rotten evening. He had only got out of the bath an hour ago but he was already scratching again.

He decided to get an early night and went to bed. He turned off the light and curled up in the dark. Justin tried to get to sleep but every time he closed his eyes his imagination went into overdrive.

He started to think
that there was
something crawling
around beside him
in the darkness. Then he became sure that
something had brushed against his feet at
the bottom of the bed. Then against his
shoulder.

He knew it was only his imagination but
finally Justin had to turn the light back on.
That was when he saw it.

There was a tiny money spider wandering aimlessly across his pillow. Justin went nuclear. He panicked and leapt out of his bed. The spider ran for safety. Justin ripped off his bedcover but he had already lost sight of it. He frantically pulled off the blanket, the sheets, and then the pillows.

He could not see
any sign of the
spider anywhere.
Where was it?
Where could
it be?

Suddenly the door opened. It was Justin's
mother, wanting to know what all the noise
was about. She was not best pleased. Justin
remade the bed under her watchful eye and
climbed back in.

30

Much later, Justin slipped into an uncomfortable sleep. But even then, he found no peace.

In his dream, Justin was the size of an ant and was being chased along a school corridor. When he looked over his shoulder, he realised that he was being hunted by massive insects.

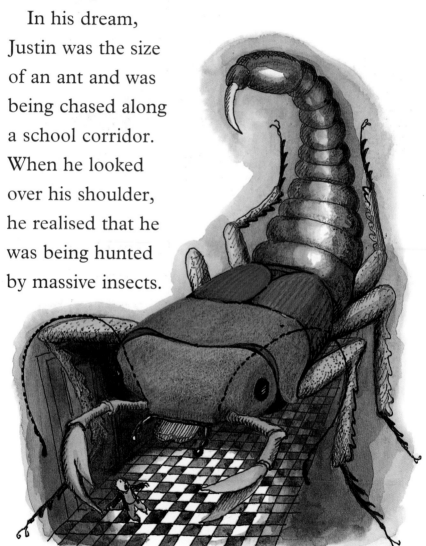

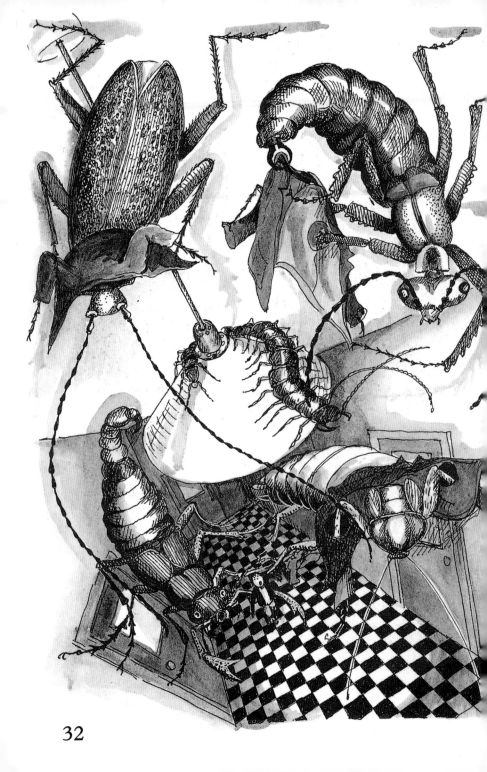

32

The dark shapes of the creatures loomed high above him. Their hard black bodies were twisting and bursting out of their school uniforms.

Wherever Justin fled, huge hairy spider legs tried to crush him. Gigantic beetle claws snapped at him at his every turn. He ran for his life.

The Bugman Hatches

In the morning, Justin woke up in a cold sweat. He lay in bed quite still. Justin knew exactly what he had to do. He quickly got dressed and left for school.

Justin had to talk to Carl. His first chance came at morning break. Carl, however, had other ideas.

When Carl saw Justin coming, he took flight. He darted back into the school building and raced down the main corridor. Justin gave chase.

Carl tried to slip into the Sports Hall, but the doors were locked. Justin began to catch up. Carl ran into the cloakroom. Surely he could lose Justin in there.

Justin entered the cloakroom and dropped to the floor. Peering under the lockers and benches he could see across the whole area. He easily spotted Carl's hiding place.

Justin advanced on Carl, who was expecting the worst.

"I need your help," said Justin. "We have to swap back."

"Swap what?" asked a confused Carl.

"You've got to take the tree project back. I mean, I've done all the work. It's nearly finished," explained Justin.

Carl was suspicious but Justin practically begged him to return his insect project. Carl left puzzled, but pleased.

Justin would have felt relieved, but he knew that the most difficult task was yet to come.

Return to the Nest

After school, Justin returned to the park but it was too crowded. He had to wait until closing time at sunset before he was alone.

As the twilight set in, Justin crept back inside. He began searching for the smashed insect nest. It was still hot and Justin was sweating all over. Justin could not find the nest. It was not where it should have been.

Justin stumbled through the darkening night. The air was humid and sticky. His eyes strained for any sign of the nest. In the distance, he heard the Park Keeper lock the gates and leave. Now he really was alone. Totally alone.

Justin went back to where his search had begun and started all over again.

There was the smashed nest. Exactly where he had looked in the first place.

Justin stared at the broken remains, his face filled with fear. The nest appeared dead and deserted. Justin knelt down on the ground. Then it began. Quickly and silently, they crawled out of the earth in front of him.

Dozens of
the weird black
bugs emerged from
the ruins of the
nest. Their long
antennae scanned the night air. They
seemed to be studying him. Justin's hands
trembled and he swallowed hard.

He leaned forward and began digging in
the earth with his bare hands. Somehow he
had to rebuild their home.

41

As he disturbed the earth, the insects began to crawl over him. Justin felt the terror in him rise but he dug harder and harder in the darkness.

He could feel some of them on his feet. Then they were in his shoes. As Justin worked, the beetles swarmed over his legs and up the spine of his back.

Justin dug as fast as he could. The bugs climbed higher and higher. Their feet pricked his skin like tiny needles.

Now they were up to his shoulders. Then on his neck. Justin pressed fists of earth onto the growing mound. He had to stifle a scream as a bug touched the side of his mouth with its multiple legs.

Justin slapped another fistful of earth onto the nest. Then another ... and another.

43

Just as he could take no more, the bugs
disappeared. Every last one of them had
turned and swarmed back into their rebuilt
home.

Justin stood up. The cooler night air hit
his sweat soaked tee-shirt and he shivered.

Justin
returned home
and collapsed, exhausted, onto his bed. As
he reached to turn out the beside lamp, he
saw a small black shape scuttle away into
the shadows. Justin smiled.

The Bugman and Friends

It was a week before Mrs Dean got around to marking the Science projects. When she gave Justin's project back, he found that he had earned an 'A'. Mrs Dean said it was excellent and that he had obviously worked very hard. He had.

After that, he became something of an expert. One day, Carl called him the Bugman. Pretty soon everyone was calling him the Bugman. Justin kind of liked it.

Three Wednesdays later, the Bugman and Carl started work on a Science project together.

They came out of school and headed for the library. As they went along, the Bugman stopped Carl just in time. "Look out! You nearly stepped on that spider," explained the anxious Bugman.

The tiny insect was allowed to escape. As the friends continued on their way, Carl noticed that the Bugman kept his eyes on the ground. Always watching where he was treading.

Look out for more creepy titles in the Shivery Storybooks series:

The Ghost Bus by Anthony Masters

When Jack and Tina catch a late bus home from school, they very quickly realise that this is no ordinary bus. For a start, it's distinctly old fashioned, but worse, they can see right through their fellow passengers! They're on a ghost bus, a ghost bus with a mission...

Little House by Herbie Brennan

When Tilly's teacher tells the class to do a drawing, Tilly draws a charming little house. But suddenly Tilly finds herself *inside* the house, and there's no door! She's trapped in her drawing. Everything she's drawn has become real, including the gigantic, evil-looking cat that has just burst into the room...

Time Flies by Mary Hooper

When Lucy hides in the wooden chest at the old manor house, it's just a game. But then she gets the fright of her life when she opens the lid and discovers that everything has changed. Somehow she has gone back to Tudor times and now she's trapped in a strange and terrifying world...

All these books and many more in the Storybooks series can be purchased from your local bookseller. For more information about Storybooks, write to: *The Sales Department, Macdonald Young Books, Campus 400, Maylands Avenue, Hemel Hempstead HP2 7EZ.*

DAVIDSON ROAD ELEMENTARY SCHOOL